TWO of a kind™

Diaries

Win tickets to
Mary-Kate and Ashley's
new movie

new york minute

Details on page 99.

Look for more

titles:

TWO of a kind™

Diaries

Prom Princess

by Diana G. Gallagher
from the series created by
Robert Griffard & Howard Adler

■HarperEntertainment
An Imprint of HarperCollinsPublishers

A PARACHUTE PRESS BOOK

A PARACHUTE PRESS BOOK

Parachute Publishing, L.L.C.
156 Fifth Avenue
Suite 302
New York, NY 10010

Published by
HarperEntertainment
An Imprint of HarperCollins*Publishers*
10 East 53rd Street, New York, NY 10022-5299

TWO OF A KIND books created and produced by
Parachute Press, L.L.C., in cooperation with Dualstar Publications,
a division of Dualstar Entertainment Group, LLC,
published by HarperEntertainment, an imprint of HarperCollins Publishers.

ISBN 0-06-009330-7

First printing: April 2004

Printed in the United States of America

Visit HarperEntertainment on the World Wide Web at
www.harpercollins.com

10 9 8 7 6 5 4 3 2 1

Chapter 1

Wednesday

Dear Diary,

Guess what! My dream of making movies might come true a lot sooner than I imagined!

I know you must be surprised, Diary. I've been keeping that a secret from you. No one except my twin sister, Mary-Kate, knows that I want to be a movie director.

Directing is *so* cool. Directors pick the stories and 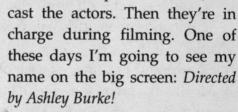 cast the actors. Then they're in charge during filming. One of these days I'm going to see my name on the big screen: *Directed by Ashley Burke!*

That's why I joined White Oak's new Young Filmmakers Club. White Oak Academy for Girls is an all-girls boarding school in New Hampshire. Mary-Kate and I are in the First Form, which is White Oak's name for seventh grade.

Today was the club's first meeting. It was held in a classroom next to the audiovisual center. I sat next to Phoebe Cahill, my roommate. While we waited, she cleaned her blue-rimmed glasses. I doodled in my notebook.

A short, chubby man walked in and stood in the front of the room. He had thin gray hair.

"Is that Alan Shanks?" Phoebe whispered. We knew that Alan Shanks was going to be the club adviser. He had worked on some big movies and TV shows.

"I guess," I whispered back.

The man didn't look like a famous movie director. I had pictured someone a lot younger with a super-hip wardrobe. This man was older than my dad and was wearing jeans, a stretched-out turtleneck, and a jacket with worn elbows.

"Good afternoon, girls," the man said. "I'm Alan Shanks."

Phoebe and I grinned at each other.

Mr. Shanks sat on the edge of the desk. "Let's talk about movies," he said. "My very first film was about my dog. I was ten, and Dusty was lost."

"Did you find him?" I asked.

"Yes," Mr. Shanks said, "ten minutes after a TV station played my video about Dusty on the news."

"That's great," Taylor Cranston said. "Your movie saved Dusty!"

"Exactly." Mr. Shanks grinned. "That's why I have made so many films and TV shows about real events. This kind of movie is called a documentary. It's a great introduction to moviemaking. And you're all going to make one! You can choose a partner or work alone."

Phoebe nudged me. "You and me—right, Ashley?"

"You bet," I said.

"I have to approve your ideas," Mr. Shanks continued, "so please pick a topic by tomorrow."

"I don't have a clue," Jessie Lang said. "What makes a good movie?"

"Choose a subject that excites you," Mr. Shanks suggested. "You'll have two weeks to write, produce, and direct a ten-minute video."

"A ten-minute movie?" Taylor said. "Aren't most movies longer than that?"

"Not all," Mr. Shanks assured us. "And ten minutes is the exact length for the student entries in the New Hampshire Film Festival." He gave us a big smile. "The best video from this club will be White Oak's student entry!"

"Cool!" I exclaimed. I glanced around. Everyone looked excited.

"What happens at a film festival?" Abigail Fitch asked.

"It's a whole weekend of films and videos," Mr. Shanks explained. "Some will be by famous people, some by newcomers. There will also be talks about movies. Many young filmmakers get their start by showing short films at festivals like this one."

He talked for a while about all the steps that go into making a good movie. Then he picked up the sign-in sheet. "That's it for today. Be ready tomorrow to tell me your movie topic."

"Let's have our own meeting," I suggested to Phoebe, "to come up with an awesome topic!"

Phoebe and I walked across the campus. We decided that I would be the director and she would run the camera. We both really wanted our video to be chosen for the film festival.

There was just one problem: We had no ideas!

"Maybe something in here will inspire us," I said as we walked into the Student Union.

A large group of girls were crowded around a table that was against the wall. They were all talking excitedly.

"This looks promising," I said. We hurried over.

"What's happening?" Phoebe asked.

"Everyone wants copies of the rules for the Prom Princess contest," Jolene Dupree explained.

The First Form Prom Princess contest is one of the biggest events of the school year, Diary. It's been a tradition since White Oak was founded—more than one hundred years ago. The Prom Princess is always a First Form student, and she is supposed to be the ideal White Oak girl. Being voted Prom Princess at the Spring Prom is a *huge* honor.

You might think it's weird that an all-girls boarding school has a prom, Diary. But boys from the nearby Harrington School for Boys take classes with us, and there are often shared activities between the two schools. The Prom Princess's date gets to be Harrington's Prom Prince!

"Are *all* these girls going to run?" I asked.

"I'm not," Jolene said. "I don't want to have to get all those signatures." She handed me a copy of the rules.

"The two girls with the most signatures by noon on Sunday will be the finalists," Holly Welsh explained.

I nodded and read the rules. Each White Oak student could nominate one—and *only* one—First Form girl. You nominated a girl by signing your name on her form. Once the two finalists were chosen, they had six days to try to convince students to vote for them. Each finalist would make a speech at an assembly for the whole school. Then everyone would vote at the dance the following Saturday. The winner would be crowned Prom Princess and become part of White Oak history.

"I'm with you, Jolene," Holly said. "I'd be scared to ask for signatures. What if everyone turned me down?" She shuddered.

"I have too much homework to run for Prom Princess," Banner Whist said. "I have a huge test in two days."

"I'll be much too busy with the video," I said.

"Me too," added Phoebe. She waved at our friends Cheryl Miller, Summer Sorenson, and Elise Van Hook to come over. They had just come into the Student Union.

"What's up?" Summer asked.

I held up the nomination form. "It's Prom Princess time!"

Elise's eyes widened. "If all these girls are running for Prom Princess, there won't be anyone left to vote!"

"I don't think they're all running," I said.

"How many signatures do I need to win?" Marsha Avery asked.

"More than the rest of us," Natalie Pittman joked.

"Are you definitely running, Natalie?" Holly asked. "Because if you are, I have to decide whose form to sign—yours or Lavender Duncan's."

"What about mine, Holly?" Marsha asked.

"Well, uh . . ." Holly shrugged. "I'm not going to

sign anyone's right now, Marsha."

"I'm running for sure," Natalie said firmly. She turned toward the door. "But right now I've got to run to softball tryouts!" She quickly left the Student Union.

"Uh, I have to go, too," Holly said. I could tell she felt uncomfortable. She wanted to get away from Marsha. Marsha frowned but didn't say anything.

Wow. This contest could get pretty serious, I realized. *A lot of girls will have to choose one friend over another for the first round of voting.*

And that's when I got the best idea!

I pulled Phoebe aside. "I have a topic for our video."

Phoebe grinned. "What is it?"

"Let's make a video about the Prom Princess contest," I said. "It's got drama, excitement, *and* suspense. All the things Mr. Shanks said a good movie should have."

"I love it!" Phoebe exclaimed. We high-fived.

So that's what we're going to do, Diary. I just hope a film about a Prom Princess contest will be good enough to enter in the New Hampshire Film Festival!

Fingers crossed!

Two of a Kind Diaries

Dear Diary,

I'm sitting in bed and I'm having a hard time staying awake to write! Softball tryouts were today. I'm tired, thrilled, and terrified!

Maybe I'd better explain that, Diary.

I'm tired because Coach Hadley worked the team really hard this afternoon. Each of us played more than one position, batted several times, and ran laps around the field. You can see why I'm so tired!

Now here's why I'm thrilled: I have a chance to break White Oak's home-run record.

Nine years ago, a girl named Jamie Jerome hit ten homers in twelve games. She was in Second Form— a grade ahead of the one I'm in. Well, I want to hit *eleven* home runs this season while I'm in *First* Form.

Ashley has known all winter about my plan. I told my roommate, Campbell Smith, today while we were waiting for tryouts to start. We were standing outside the dugout because the bench inside was full.

"You'll have to hit a home run every game, Mary-Kate," Campbell said, her brown eyes very serious.

"*Almost* every game," I corrected her. "There are

twelve games in a season, but I only need eleven to beat Jamie Jerome's record."

"No problem." Campbell grinned. "If anyone at White Oak can do it, you can."

"Do what?" Dana Woletsky asked as she came up behind us. I noticed her cashmere sweater matched her green eyes and her brown corduroy miniskirt matched her hair. She was carrying a notebook.

Why is Dana here? I wondered. I knew it couldn't be good. Dana never misses a chance to make my life miserable.

"Mary-Kate wants to break—" Campbell started to answer Dana's question.

I cut her off. "Are you trying out for the team, Dana?" I didn't want anyone to know about my secret goal—especially Dana!

"I'm covering the softball season for the *Acorn*," Dana explained. The *White Oak Acorn* is the school newspaper. Dana is one of its editors.

"That's nice," I said. I don't like Dana, but I try not to be rude. It's not easy, Diary!

"So what are you going to break, Mary-Kate?" Dana asked again.

"Jamie Jerome's home-run record," Natalie Pittman

said as she stepped out of the dugout. She must have heard Campbell and me talking.

"Great. I'll put that in my newspaper story," Dana said. She flipped open her notebook and started taking notes.

Oh, no! I stared at Dana. *Now everyone will know I'm trying to break the school home-run record. Talk about pressure!*

Coach Hadley blew her whistle to start the practice. She divided the players into two groups. One group ran onto the field. Campbell and I were in the first group to bat.

I love stepping up to the plate. I'm small, but I've got a good eye and a strong swing. I can usually tune out everything except the ball.

Today all I could feel was Dana staring at me.

Rachel Delmar's first pitch was right over the plate. I swung—and missed!

"What? Mary-Kate missed?" Dana exclaimed, surprised. "Now *that's* news!" She scribbled something in her notebook.

"Don't worry about it, Mary-Kate," Campbell called.

I took a deep breath and tightened my grip on the bat. I couldn't let Dana psych me out. I swung at the next pitch and hit a grounder.

"What kind of lame hit was *that*, Mary-Kate?"

Dana yelled as I ran to first base. I stopped and glared at her.

"I don't think Jamie Jerome has to worry about anyone breaking her home-run record *this* year," Dana called across the field.

So that's why I'm terrified: Dana is going to blab it all over school that I'm trying to beat the record.

And I have no idea if I can!

Chapter 2

Thursday

Dear Diary,

Ashley and I sat together at lunch. My sister had to present her Prom Princess video idea to Mr. Shanks later today.

"So far only Marsha Avery, Lavender Duncan, and Natalie Pittman are entering the contest," Ashley said.

"Only three?" I asked, surprised.

"A lot of girls are worried about competing," Ashley explained.

"Competition won't bother Natalie," I said. "I've seen her play basketball and softball!"

Ashley nodded. "I think Natalie likes to compete almost as much as she likes to win." She crumpled her juice carton. "How did tryouts go?"

"Okay, I guess," I said, frowning.

I didn't want to admit that Dana's taunts had thrown me off my game, but I share everything with Ashley. She would know that something was bothering me.

"Dana found out that I want to break the school home-run record," I explained. "She's going to write about it in the *Acorn*. Now everyone will know."

"That might not be so bad," Ashley said. "Everyone will be cheering you on."

"Everyone except Dana Woletsky," I said. "She can't wait to tell the whole school that I can't break the record."

"But you can!" Ashley said. "You're the best hitter on the team."

I smiled. My sister totally believes in me, Diary. It feels great!

"I'll catch you later, Mary-Kate." Ashley stood up. "I've got to write up my video idea."

I finished my strawberry yogurt. When I walked out of the dining hall I walked right into the middle of an argument—between Natalie and Dana! Kristen Lindquist and Brooke Miller were standing off to the side. They didn't look very happy.

"No fair, Natalie," Dana said. Her face was red.

"It's totally fair, Dana," Natalie shot back. She turned to me. "What do you think, Mary-Kate?"

"About what?" I asked, stepping between them. That, Diary, was my first mistake.

Dana put her hands on her hips. "Kristen and Brooke are my best friends," she declared.

I glanced at Kristen and Brooke. Kristen stared at her shoes. Brooke bit her lip.

"Okay," I agreed. "And this is a problem because . . . "

"Because Kristen and Brooke already signed *my* nomination form," Natalie said.

"We didn't know Dana was going to run for Prom Princess, Mary-Kate," Brooke explained.

"I decided at the last minute," Dana huffed.

Kristen looked up from her shoes. "If we had known you were going to run, Dana, we wouldn't have signed Natalie's form. Honest."

I could tell Kristen and Brooke were upset. Dana is the leader of White Oak's snobby crowd. Signing Natalie's form instead of Dana's for Prom Princess was a really bad move for Brooke and Kristen.

"Cross Kristen's and Brooke's names off your form right now, Natalie," Dana demanded. Her voice got louder. "So they can sign mine."

"Once you've signed someone's form, you can't change your mind and sign someone else's form instead," Natalie insisted. Her voice got louder, too.

I did *not* want to be in the middle of Dana and Natalie's problem. I had no idea how to solve it! I was glad when Mrs. Weinstock, the dining hall supervisor, interrupted.

"What's going on here?" Mrs. Weinstock asked.

Natalie, Dana, Kristen, Brooke, and I all began talking at once.

"Natalie's being a jerk," Dana snapped.

"I am not!" Natalie's temper flared. "You are!"

"It's all our fault," Brooke said.

"But we didn't know," Kristen added.

"It's just a misunderstanding," I said.

"Enough!" Mrs. Weinstock held up her hands. "Since you girls can't settle your differences peacefully, we'll let Mrs. Pritchard do it."

Great, I thought as Mrs. Weinstock pointed toward the Administration Building. Ashley has told me a thousand times to mind my own business, Diary. Next time I'll listen.

The five of us formed a line in front of Mrs. Pritchard's desk. The headmistress smoothed her short silver hair. Her rhinestone glasses were hanging on a chain around her neck. "What seems to be the problem?" she asked.

"Natalie won't let Brooke and Kristen sign my Prom Princess nomination form," Dana said.

"Because they already signed mine!" Natalie cried.

"Only because we didn't know Dana was running," Brooke protested.

"That's right," Kristen said.

"Why are you here, Mary-Kate?" Mrs. Pritchard asked.

"Natalie, uh, asked my opinion," I explained. "But I don't really have one."

"I see." Mrs. Pritchard sat back and folded her hands.

Everyone waited. That was a *long* minute.

"I'm sorry, Dana, but I have to agree with Natalie about this," Mrs. Pritchard said. "No crossing out of names after signing. That would be too confusing."

"But Kristen and Brooke are my friends," Dana said.

"I understand, Dana," Mrs. Pritchard said. "But if I let them change their votes, then I have to let other girls change their votes, too. If too many people start switching at the last minute, it will be a mess. We might even have girls signing more than one form."

Mrs. Pritchard stood and showed us out her door. "Good-bye, girls," she said. Then she turned her attention to another girl waiting to see her.

As soon as we got into the hall, Natalie shot Dana a smug look and hurried away.

"We're sorry, Dana," Kristen murmured.

"We really do want to sign your form," Brooke added.

"Forget it," Dana snapped. "This is all Mary-Kate's fault."

"Why is it my fault?" I asked. Somehow Dana always makes me the bad guy. It's amazing.

"You could have just told Natalie to let me have Kristen's and Brooke's signatures, Mary-Kate, but *nooooo*." Dana rolled her eyes.

"Do you really think Natalie would have agreed just because I said so, Dana?" I asked.

Dana was too angry to listen. "I won't forget this, Mary-Kate."

I hate to say this, Diary, because I know it's not nice, but I sure hope Dana doesn't become our school Prom Princess!

Dear Diary,

I've got the green light for the Prom Princess video! That's what they say in Hollywood when a project is approved. And Mr. Shanks made a suggestion to make the video even better.

"Make one of the contestants the 'star' of your video," he said. "Audiences care more about someone they can get to know."

That's a great idea, I thought. *But which contestant?*

Mr. Shanks handed out the digital video cameras we were going to use and explained how they worked. After the meeting Phoebe and I raced back to our room. Phoebe sat cross-legged on her bed and read the whole instruction book cover to cover.

I labeled a spiral notebook with the name of our project. I wanted to keep a record of every shot.

"Okay, Madame Director, what do we do first?" Phoebe asked.

I picked up the notebook and a pen. "We find our star!"

Since it was dinnertime, Phoebe and I headed straight for the dining hall. Phoebe was going to videotape my interviews with all the Prom Princess contestants. We could decide later which shots to use, once we decided who the star of our video was going to be.

I spotted Marsha Avery sitting on a bench outside the dining hall.

"Hey, Ashley!" Marsha said, holding out a clipboard and a pen. "Do you want to sign my Prom Princess form?"

"Not right now," I said. I planned to sign for the girl who starred in my video. So did Mary-Kate, Campbell, and Phoebe. "I'm making a video about the Prom Princess contest—"

"You are?" Marsha interrupted, frowning at the camera. "Now?"

Marsha looked upset. Maybe she was worried about her hair or her outfit. I tried to make her calm. "These shots don't have to be in it," I said.

"I don't want to be in it at all!" Marsha exclaimed.

"You don't?" I was surprised. I thought having a video crew follow you everywhere would be fun.

Marsha stared down at her clipboard. "I only have eight signatures," she whispered. "If I lose, I don't want to be totally embarrassed in a video."

I could see her point. "I understand," I said. I spotted Lavender Duncan going into the dining hall. "Catch you later," I told Marsha.

Phoebe and I followed Lavender across the dining room. We waited until she went through the dinner line and sat at a table near the window. She was fluffing her short brown hair as I stopped at her table.

"Hey, Lavender," I said, "can I sit down?"

"Sure!" Lavender smiled brightly, and her gray eyes sparkled. "What's up?"

I saw the nomination form clipped to Lavender's notebook. Most of the lines on Lavender's form were filled in. She was doing much better than Marsha.

"I'm making a movie about the Prom Princess contest," I said. "Do you want to be in it?"

"Me?" Lavender looked confused. "Why me?"

"Uh . . ." I didn't have a good answer. Phoebe and I had just asked the first two contestants we saw. I pointed to Lavender's binder. "Your nomination form is almost full," I said.

"True," Lavender said. "All my friends signed for me this morning. But I don't think it will be enough to make me a finalist."

"You still have time to ask for more signatures, don't you?" I asked.

Lavender shrugged. "I don't think I can ask girls I don't know! I get tongue-tied when I have to answer questions out loud in class." She looked past me and gasped. "Is that camera on?" she asked, pointing at Phoebe.

"Yes, it is," I said. I suddenly had a good interview idea. I waved for Phoebe to move closer. "Can you tell me why you want to be the Prom Princess, Lavender?"

"You want me to talk? To the camera?" Lavender's gray eyes widened. Her mouth dropped open a little.

"Lavender?" I leaned closer. "Are you okay?"

Lavender didn't answer. She just stared at the camera.

"I'm turning it off," Phoebe said. She pressed the pause button and lowered the camera.

Lavender let out a long, slow breath. Then she smiled at me. "Sorry, Ashley. I'm just not good at this sort of thing."

"That's okay," I said. "Good luck with the contest."

"Now what?" Phoebe asked as we walked toward an empty table.

"Let's hope we have better luck with Natalie," I said. "Because I do *not* want Dana to be our star!"

Phoebe and I caught up with Natalie after dinner in the Student Union. She was playing a video game. After she scored, I quickly explained my video project.

"You want to videotape *everything* I do?" Natalie asked.

"Yes," I said. "I'm going to tape the whole contest from start to finish."

"That sounds like fun," she said. "But if I say yes, I have a few rules. No taping while I'm eating." She wrinkled her nose. "Nobody looks good when they're chewing."

Natalie had a point, but I suddenly had a bad feeling about her being my star.

"No taping without telling me," Natalie went on. "And I get to choose which shots of me you can use."

I could tell it would be tricky to work with her.

"We'll let you know if we decide to cast you, Natalie," Phoebe said. She shut off the camera and slapped the screen closed. "Right, Ashley?" She shot me a look that said *"No way!"*

"Right," I said. I grabbed Phoebe's arm and hurried her away. I knew Natalie wouldn't be our star. But now we didn't *have* a star!

Phoebe and I sat on a bench outside our dorm, Porter House. "There's only one person left," Phoebe said.

I shook my head. "I absolutely will *not* ask Dana to star in our video."

"Okay—but who then?" Phoebe asked. She shrugged. "Maybe Marsha will change her mind."

"Maybe," I said. "But eight nominations aren't enough to make her a finalist."

"I'll sign for you, Ashley," Amber Fleming said, passing by. She stopped in front of me and pulled a pen out of her bag. "Do you have your form with you?"

"My form?" I said, confused.

"For the Prom Princess contest," Amber said. "I think it would be awesome if you won."

"Oh, no." I shook my head. "I'm not running for Prom Princess. I'm just making a video about it."

Phoebe looked up sharply.

"Well, let me know if you change your mind," Amber said and waved as she walked away.

Phoebe was staring at me.

"What?" I said.

"You should star in the video, Ashley," Phoebe said. She picked up the camera and pointed it straight at me.

"Me?" My mouth dropped open.

"All our friends would nominate you in a second," Phoebe said. "Lots of other girls would, too. You're the only hope for our video."

"I don't know . . ." I said.

"Remember," Phoebe added, "it's you or Dana."

That decided it. "Me," I declared.

And that, Diary, means I have to run for Prom Princess!

Chapter 3

Friday

Dear Diary,

Now that I'm running for Prom Princess, I realize how cool it would be to win!

There's more to being Prom Princess than just the tiara. First of all, it's a big honor. It means girls in all the grades think you are the ideal White Oak stu-dent: well-rounded, smart, kind, loyal, and fun! And, Diary, once a Prom Princess, always a Prom Princess. The former Prom Princesses have a welcoming party for the new one. There's even a newsletter sent around by grown-up Prom Princesses.

Just imagine, Diary, when I'm ninety-nine years old I could be telling some future First Form girl what it was like to be a Prom Princess.

If I win, of course!

"You're up early." Phoebe sat up and stretched.

"Excited, I guess," I said. I put aside my diary and picked up the spiral notebook. "And nervous. We're going to need a really great video if we want ours to be chosen for the film festival!"

Phoebe nodded and ran her hands through her curly brown hair. "The other girls came up with some awesome ideas."

It's true, Diary. Jessie Lang and Alyssa Fuji are videotaping a department store's makeover of a girl, and then seeing if people treat the girl differently after her makeover. Abigail Fitch's video is about roommates. Taylor Cranston and Ellen Withers are going to show what it's like to be a teacher at White Oak. Blair Clark's video is called *The Life and Death of a Green Bean*. Now that's not too exciting—is it, Diary?

"I have an idea how to start," I told Phoebe.

"Let's hear it," Phoebe said.

I swiveled my chair to face her. "Our first scene should be about the contest. We can use shots of the other girls getting signatures, with my voice explaining the rules. We'll end that part when I decide to run."

"I love it!" Phoebe beamed. "We have all the contestants on camera except for Dana. I'll film her today."

"Next we'll tape me collecting signatures," I said.

"We need to get some signatures at breakfast," Phoebe said, jumping out of bed. "Everyone else has a major head start. Even Dana!"

I had been so busy planning the video, I hadn't

thought about how much work we had to do for the contest. Our video would be a total flop if I didn't make it as a finalist!

We got showered and dressed. Just before leaving for breakfast, I put the Prom Princess form on a clipboard.

"Wait!" Phoebe said. She turned the camera on and handed it to me.

"What are you doing?" I asked as she picked up a pen.

"Film this," she said. She made a big show of signing her name on the top line. "Your first nomination," she said.

"Now it's official!" I said, giggling.

We left the room and ran into Tammi Patterson coming down the hall. Phoebe stood back with the camera running.

"Hi, Tammi!" I said. "I just decided to run for Prom Princess. Will you sign my form?"

"You'd be perfect, Ashley," Tammi said. "But I signed Dana's form last night."

"Oh," I said. I tried not to look disappointed. Phoebe was still taping. And I didn't want Tammi to feel bad.

"I'm really sorry, Ashley," Tammi said. Then she pointed toward the stairs. Layne Wagner and

Carmen Barnes were just starting down. "Maybe they'll sign for you."

"Thanks." I hurried over to Layne and Carmen. Phoebe jogged after me with the camera. On the second floor we caught up with the two girls. "Hi, guys!"

"Hey, Ashley!" Carmen smiled. "What's up?"

"I decided to run for Prom Princess," I said. "Will you sign my form?"

"I can't," Layne said. "I already voted for Lavender."

"Me too," Carmen said.

"I understand," I said. Both girls were good friends with Lavender. I forced a smile. "See you later."

Phoebe and I waited until Layne and Carmen had gone.

"Don't worry, Ashley," Phoebe said. "I know for a fact that Summer and Elise haven't signed for anyone yet."

I was glad to hear that, but Summer Sorenson and Elise Van Hook were only two people. I needed more signatures than that!

That's why I'm worried, Diary. What if everyone I know has already nominated someone else? Is it too late?

Two of a Kind Diaries

Dear Diary,

"Wow! Ashley has fifty signatures!" I exclaimed.

"Awesome," Campbell said.

We were sitting on the bleachers by the dugout. The rest of the team was hanging out, waiting for Coach Hadley. She was announcing our positions today.

I promised Ashley I would ask the girls on the softball team to sign her form. Summer and Elise were collecting signatures for her at the library while Ashley went to her Young Filmmakers Club meeting.

"That's amazing." Campbell was impressed. "She started two days late!"

My sister might actually win, I realized. I hoped so. Now that Ashley had entered the contest, she really wanted to be Prom Princess.

"I'll sign it." Campbell took my pen and signed the form.

"I want to nominate Ashley, too," our teammate, Sonya Perez, said. She took the pen and clipboard from Campbell.

"Wait a minute!" Dana said, walking out of the dugout. "Sonya, you said you'd sign for me!"

I groaned inside. I had forgotten that Dana would be at the field to hear Coach Hadley's announcement for her newspaper article.

"Well, I said that before I knew Ashley was running," Sonya said.

"That's just great!" Dana glared at me, then stalked back into the dugout.

"Is she still mad at you?" Campbell asked.

"Dana is *always* mad at me," I said. "Or maybe she's upset because she isn't getting as many signatures as she expected."

I collected several other signatures. Dana sat in the dugout, watching everything with a frown.

Natalie came up from behind me. "Ashley is doing pretty great, huh?" she said, looking over my shoulder.

"So far," I said. I glanced at the clipboard and realized that the top sheet was completely filled!

"I want you to know I'm not upset that most of the softball team signed for Ashley," Natalie said. "I already have more than enough signatures to be a finalist."

"That's great," I said. I wondered how she could know that she had enough names. Had she counted everyone's signatures?

"Okay, girls!" Coach Hadley called from the field.

I pressed the metal clip on the board and slid a blank nomination form on top.

Natalie dropped her clipboard. Her pages fell out when the clipboard hit the ground. "Oops!" She stooped to pick up the loose papers.

"Come on, Mary-Kate!" Campbell waved me onto the field. "Coach is going to announce our positions!"

I left Ashley's clipboard on the seat and dashed to join my teammates. I hoped Coach Hadley would assign me to first base!

Natalie ran to the dugout and put her clipboard away. Then she joined the rest of us on the field.

"White Oak is going to have a great team this year," Coach Hadley began. "Everyone played so well at tryouts it was hard to decide which positions you should play."

I heard footsteps on the bleachers. Dana had left the dugout and was now sitting on the bleachers. But she wasn't taking notes for the newspaper. She was flipping through the nomination forms on Ashley's clipboard.

I felt my face grow hot. I couldn't say or do *anything*—not during practice.

Coach assigned us to our positions—and I got my wish: first base! Then we started the game. I was up at bat first. I glanced back at the bleachers again.

Great. Now Dana was staring straight at me. She had her notebook on her lap and her pen in her hand.

This one is for you, Dana. I gripped the bat. *I'm going to hit this over the fence.*

I swung—and gasped! Pain shot through my arm, and I dropped the bat. I bit my lip trying to fight back tears. My arm *burned!*

Oh, no! I thought as Coach ran over. *Will I still be able to play softball?*

Chapter 4

Saturday

Dear Diary,

Summer and Elise saved seats in the dining hall for me and Phoebe. We got there a little late because of our Young Filmmakers Club meeting. Mr. Shanks gave us more pointers, and everyone talked about how they were making their videos. It was fun—and inspiring!

And I even got three more signatures from girls in the club!

"Elise and I got ten signatures at the library for you," Summer said. She took a bite of her veggie lasagna.

"Really?" I was impressed. "That's great."

"How many signatures do you have now, Ashley?" Elise asked.

"I'm not sure," I said. "That depends on how many Mary-Kate got at softball practice." I glanced around the dining hall, but I didn't see Mary-Kate anywhere. "Where is she?"

"I don't know," Phoebe said. Then she pointed at the door. "But here comes Campbell."

"Where's Mary-Kate?" I asked when Campbell sat down.

"Mary-Kate hurt her arm at softball practice,"

Campbell explained. "The nurse sent her back to our room."

"Is she okay?" I stood up and started gathering my stuff. I had to go check on my sister!

"You can sit down, Ashley," Campbell said. "She's fine. She just has to rest her arm."

"Will Mary-Kate be able to play in the first game next week?" Summer asked.

"The nurse just said Mary-Kate can't practice for a few days," Campbell explained.

I groaned. "Mary-Kate is *not* going to like that!" My sister was really psyched about trying to beat that home-run record. Being benched was not going to make her very happy!

After dinner, Campbell, Phoebe, and I went to check on Mary-Kate. She was sitting on her bed holding an ice pack on her upper arm. She looked really glad to see us. "Hey, guys!"

"How are you doing?" I asked. "Campbell told us you got hurt at practice."

"Not great," Mary-Kate admitted. "The nurse said I pulled a muscle. But"—she grinned—"I got lots of signatures for you!"

"Super!" I smiled. I handed Mary-Kate a bowl of

macaroni I brought for her from the dining hall.

"Should we film me counting the nominations?" I asked Phoebe.

"Good idea!" she said and reached for the camera.

I unfolded the form I used at the Young Filmmakers Club meeting and the one I had given Summer to use at the library. "I have to add these to the whole collection," I said.

"Your clipboard is on my desk," Mary-Kate said.

"So how many do you have total, Ashley?" Phoebe asked from behind the camera.

"Sixty-three plus the ten softball players equals seventy-three!" I grinned. "Is that enough to make me a finalist?"

"I hope so," Mary-Kate said.

"Me too," Campbell added.

"Hold up all the sheets so I can videotape them," Phoebe suggested.

"Okay." I pressed the metal clip on the clipboard and removed the pages. There were two blank forms under the page Mary-Kate had filled up. But the two pages I had filled up weren't there. "Mary-Kate, where are my other two pages I filled up?"

"What do you mean?" Mary-Kate asked. "Aren't they on the clipboard?"

I looked again. And then again. But no matter

how many times I flipped through the pages, it came out the same each time.

My votes weren't there.

Dear Diary,

What happened to Ashley's signatures?

"The sheets have to be here somewhere," I said. I started to panic. As soon as I moved, though, a pain in my arm made me yelp!

"You stay still," Campbell ordered me. "We'll look."

Ashley, Campbell, and Phoebe searched the room. Phoebe looked in the wastebasket and under my bed. Ashley went through all of my desk drawers. Campbell checked the closet and the dresser. They searched anyplace a piece of paper could be hiding.

Ashley looked really upset, and I didn't blame her. I was upset, too—since I was the one who lost her signatures: forty of them!

"Those pages didn't just disappear," Phoebe said.

"Think back, Mary-Kate," Ashley said. "When was the last time you saw them?"

I bit my lip, trying to remember. "The pages were on the clipboard when Campbell signed," I said. "I had just counted them. Then Lexy Martin and eight other softball players signed."

"And that filled up the third form," Campbell added.

"So I pulled out a new form," I said. "Maybe that's when the pages dropped out! They're probably under the bleachers."

"Let's go look," Ashley said.

I wasn't going to stay in my room while they searched. I carefully put on my 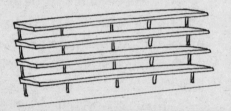 jacket, and then Campbell, Phoebe, Ashley, and I hurried to the softball field. It was starting to get dark, but we searched everywhere.

We didn't find Ashley's nomination forms.

"Do you have enough signatures to be a Prom Princess finalist without the missing sheets?" Campbell asked.

Ashley shook her head. "I don't think so. I'll only have thirty-three votes."

Phoebe looked through a trash container by the bleachers. "No nomination forms in here."

"Well, I'm not going to give up," I said. "Maybe someone on the softball team saw what happened to them."

Campbell looked at her watch. "It's almost curfew. We'd better hurry if we want to ask them tonight."

Ashley and Phoebe left to search the path from the field to Porter House. Campbell and I ran to Phipps House, another dorm.

Not a single girl we asked from the softball team knew anything about the missing forms.

"That's everyone in this house," I said.

"Except Dana," Campbell said. "She was at the field working on her article for the *Acorn*."

I gasped. "I saw Dana looking through Ashley's clipboard when Coach Hadley announced the positions."

"Do you think Dana *took* Ashley's forms?" Campbell asked.

"I don't know," I said. "She didn't look too happy when she flipped through Ashley's pages."

Diary, did Dana want to be Prom Princess so badly, she'd steal someone else's nomination forms?

Chapter 5

Sunday

Dear Diary,

I wish I had better news to report, but I don't. Phoebe and I looked everywhere between the softball field and Porter House last night. We couldn't find my missing forms. No one Mary-Kate asked has seen them, either.

Right before curfew Phoebe and I found three girls who had signed the missing forms. When I told them what had happened, they signed my new form. But that's only three out of forty!

Today Phoebe and I tried to find more girls who had signed my lost pages. The deadline was noon! My chance of being a finalist was slipping away.

"Are you sure you want me to keep taping?" Phoebe asked.

I nodded. "We need a movie for the Young Filmmakers Club, even if it's about *losing* the Prom Princess contest."

Susanna Worley came out of the Student Union. "Susanna!" I called.

Susanna was happy to nominate me again. We ran into two other girls heading for the Harrington School for Boys' lacrosse team practice on our school's field. They signed for me a second time, too.

"Maybe there will be some more girls at practice," I said. We headed for the playing field.

"Hey, there's Ross!" Phoebe exclaimed.

Ross Lambert is my boyfriend. He's really smart and totally cute. I hadn't seen Ross much the past week because the Harrington lacrosse team had been practicing every day for the county finals.

"Hi, Ashley!" Ross ran to the edge of the field. He pointed to my clipboard. "Are you still collecting signatures?"

"I've got half an hour before I have to hand them in," I said.

"Move closer together, you two!" Phoebe waved her hand and aimed the camera.

Ross put his arm around my shoulders and smiled. "The prom is going to be fun. I've never danced with a Princess before."

"I have to win the contest first," I reminded him.

"How can you miss, Ashley?" Ross said. He gave me a sly grin. "Especially when you've got *me* as your Prince?" He winked at the camera.

I gave him a playful punch on the arm. Then the

coach called him back onto the lacrosse field.

"That will be one of the best scenes in the whole movie!" Phoebe declared. She checked her watch. "We'd better go hand in your forms."

Phoebe and I arrived at the Administration Building at eleven-fifty exactly. Phoebe kept filming.

Dana rushed toward us.

"Smile, Dana!" Phoebe said. "You're on camera!"

Dana just scowled.

"How many signatures did you get?" I asked.

"That's my business, not yours." Dana clutched her forms to her chest and hurried through the door.

Phoebe lowered the camera. "What's her problem?"

"I don't know," I said. Then it hit me. The one explanation for Dana's bad mood.

Maybe Dana didn't have very many signatures.

Which meant I might still have a chance to be a Prom Princess finalist!

Dear Diary,

I asked myself questions all night! Did I drop Ashley's forms? I don't know. Did Dana find them? I don't know. Did she take the sheets off the clipboard? I don't know.

Still, I had a very funny feeling that Dana had my

sister's nomination forms. But I couldn't prove it.

At dinner tonight Ashley told Summer and Elise about the missing forms.

"What rotten luck, Ashley," Elise said. "You worked so hard to get all those signatures."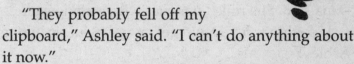

"You don't know what happened to them?" Summer asked.

"They probably fell off my clipboard," Ashley said. "I can't do anything about it now."

I smiled at my sister. She hadn't told anyone that it was my fault her pages were lost.

Dana, Kristen, Brooke, and Lisa Dunmead stopped at the table next to us. "Let's sit over here," Dana declared. She walked around to the far side of the table. Kristen, Brooke, and Lisa followed her. "I don't want Mary-Kate's losing streak to rub off on me."

"What losing streak?" Kristen asked.

"You know how Mary-Kate wants to break the home-run record?" Dana said. "Well, she can't bat now that she hurt her arm!"

My cheeks burned, but I kept quiet. Dana was right—which made me feel even worse.

"Losing runs in Mary-Kate's family this week," Dana went on.

"It does?" Lisa said.

Dana nodded. "I don't think Ashley has much chance of being a Prom Princess finalist."

Ashley's head snapped up.

No one knew what to say—except me. I turned to face Dana. "What makes you so sure Ashley doesn't have a chance?" I asked.

"Oh, come on now. Ashley started *two* days late," Dana said. She rolled her eyes with a smug smile.

I couldn't let Dana get away with insulting Ashley!

I was so angry, Diary, that before I could think about what I was saying, I blurted out, "I know what you did, Dana. I know you stole Ashley's nomination forms!"

Chapter 6

Sunday

Dear Diary,

I couldn't believe my ears. Mary-
Kate accused Dana Woletsky of *stealing*
my nomination forms!

Everyone at our table was stunned. The whole
dining hall got quiet.

"Are you calling me a thief, Mary-Kate?" Dana
said, looking shocked.

"If the name fits, Dana," Mary-Kate shot back.

"You know," Campbell said, "I saw Dana looking at the clipboard Mary-Kate left on the bleachers
yesterday."

Phoebe gasped. "Is that why
you wouldn't show Ashley
your nomination forms at the
Administration Building today,
Dana?" She kept the camera
rolling. "Because you knew
Ashley would recognize the
names of girls who voted for *her*?"

"No!" Dana shook her head. "I didn't want to tell
because I didn't want to jinx my chances."

"Do you expect us to believe that, Dana?"
Campbell asked.

"I believe it," Brooke said.

"Me too," Kristen said. Lisa nodded.

"Well, I don't," Cheryl Miller said from another table. "Dana was mad because I signed Ashley's form instead of hers."

Summer glared at Dana. "Taking someone else's forms is really low, Dana."

"I didn't do anything," Dana insisted. "And you can't prove that I did."

I looked around the dining hall. It was obvious from all the whispering and pointing that Dana's closest friends were the only ones who believed her story.

That won't help me, though, Diary. The nomination forms have already been turned in. And Dana will get credit for my signatures!

Dear Diary,

Coach Hadley called me into her office right before my P.E. class was about to begin.

"I spoke to the nurse, Mary-Kate," Coach said. "She doesn't want you to play any sports until our first game on Friday."

"Why not?" I asked.

"So your arm can heal," the coach explained.

"My arm feels fine." I swung my arm around to

prove it. It was a little stiff, but it didn't hurt. "I'll lose my batting edge if I don't practice for four days!"

"It won't take you long to get your edge back," Coach Hadley said.

"But I have to bat my *best* on Friday," I explained. "I'm trying to break the home-run record. I can't do that if I don't practice."

"You won't break *any* records if your injury gets worse, Mary-Kate," the coach pointed out.

We were interrupted by a knock on the door. Dana stuck her head inside. "Excuse me, Coach Hadley," she said. "I came to pick up the Mighty Oaks' game schedule for the *Acorn*."

"I'll be with you in a moment, Dana," Coach Hadley said.

"Okay," Dana said and stepped back into the hall.

Coach looked back at me. "You are not to practice softball until the nurse checks your arm on Friday morning, Mary-Kate—or I'll have to bench you for the game, too."

"Okay, Coach," I said. I could tell it wouldn't do any good to argue.

"You can do homework in the library during P.E. today," Coach Hadley said.

Dana glared at me as I left. I ignored her. I didn't

care if she was mad at me for telling everyone she had taken Ashley's signatures.

I headed toward the library with my glove, ball, and books.

My arm felt stiff. I bent and straightened it a few times. That seemed to help a bit. *I don't have to bat to keep my arm in shape*, I realized. *I just have to work the muscles.*

And I can do that right here! I stopped at the back door of the library. I set down my books and slipped on my glove.

I threw the ball at the brick building and caught it when it bounced back. My arm felt tight, but after a while it started to loosen up.

"What are you doing, Mary-Kate?" Dana asked from behind me. Her voice took me by surprise.

"Going to the library," I said, turning to face Dana. I hid my glove behind my back. The softball bounced off the building and hit the ground. It rolled past me toward Dana.

"No, you're not, Mary-Kate. You're practicing!" Dana exclaimed as she picked up the ball. "I just heard Coach Hadley tell you *not* to practice!"

I couldn't believe that *Dana* had caught me!

"Where are you going?" I asked when she turned and started walking away with my ball.

"To tell Coach Hadley you were practicing!" she yelled back over her shoulder.

Oh, no! Will Coach Hadley really bench me so I can't play in Friday's game? If she does, I fumed, *it will be because of Dana!*

Dear Diary,

I was drawing a still life of fruit when Layne Wagner came into my art class today. She handed the teacher a note.

"Ashley," Ms. Keech said, "Mrs. Pritchard would like to see you in her office."

"Me?" I squeaked. Getting called out of class to see the headmistress is serious stuff! Everyone in the class stopped working to stare at me.

I took off my smock and hung it up. Then I grabbed my books.

"Ashley never gets in trouble!" Wendy whispered to Jolene as I walked by.

"I wonder what she did," Jolene whispered back.

Me too! I thought as I left.

My stomach was in knots when I got to the office. I couldn't figure out what I had done wrong.

The secretary pointed toward Mrs. Pritchard's door. "Go on in, Ashley."

My hand shook on the doorknob when I opened the door. I was surprised to see Natalie Pittman sitting across from Mrs. Pritchard's desk.

Are we both in trouble? I wondered as I walked inside. My head was spinning. I hate not knowing what's going on.

"Have a seat, Ashley," Mrs. Pritchard said.

I sat down with my books in my lap and folded my hands on top of them.

"We have a problem with your Prom Princess nomination forms," Mrs. Pritchard said. "I want to explain it so that there's no misunderstanding."

"What kind of problem?" I asked.

"The same eight girls signed nomination forms for both of you," Mrs. Pritchard explained.

"Eight?" I repeated the word. My mind did some quick math. Eight girls had signed for me a second time between Saturday night and Sunday noon.

"A student cannot nominate two people. That's the rule," the headmistress said. "We'll be subtracting those eight names from each of your totals."

"That seems fair," Natalie said.

I just stared. A terrible truth suddenly became

clear: The only way there could be any duplication would be if Natalie had taken my forms.

Natalie cheated.

And Dana hadn't!

What should I do? I wondered. *This isn't fair at all!*

Natalie wouldn't lose much if eight nominations were taken away from her total. She had my *other* thirty-two signers!

I had to tell the truth.

"Hmmm . . . well—" I tried to begin, but Mrs. Pritchard wasn't finished.

"I don't think anyone meant to break the rules," Mrs. Pritchard continued. "I'm sure the girls who signed twice just didn't want to say 'No' to a friend."

"Probably not," Natalie said, smiling at the headmistress. She didn't look at me.

"Actually, that's not—" I started. Then I stopped.

At school, being a tattletale was almost as bad as being a thief. I couldn't rat out Natalie.

"It's a good thing nobody cheated," Mrs. Pritchard said. "I'd have to cancel the Prom Princess contest. That's never happened before."

That made me glad I hadn't said anything. I

didn't want to be responsible for ending the Prom Princess contest—not after it has been a tradition for over one hundred years!

"Are we good here, girls?" Mrs. Pritchard stood and opened her door for us.

"I'm okay with it," Natalie said, standing up. "How about you, Ashley?" She looked straight at me.

"I'm fine, too," I said, meeting her stare. "Just fine."

"Excellent. I'm glad we're done with that problem," Mrs. Pritchard said as she left the office. Natalie and I followed her out.

This isn't done, Natalie, I thought. *Not between us this isn't. There is no way I'm letting you be Prom Princess.*

Chapter 7

Monday

Dear Diary,

I was so angry with Natalie, I couldn't get anything done. In class I kept daydreaming that Natalie won the Prom Princess contest and I ran up onto the stage and snatched the glittering tiara off her head!

And worst of all, I couldn't talk to anyone about it! Mary-Kate had softball practice, and Phoebe had a dentist appointment. I had to wait until I saw them at dinner.

But at dinner Cheryl, Lexy, Summer, and Elise sat down with us, too. I wanted to tell Mary-Kate and Phoebe what had happened, but there were too many people around.

Besides, Mary-Kate had a problem, too.

"Coach Hadley benched you?" Campbell asked.

Mary-Kate nodded. "The nurse said I couldn't practice until Friday. I was just throwing a ball, trying to keep my arm limber, but Dana saw me and told Coach Hadley."

"Dana should know that the Mighty Oaks have a

better chance of winning if *you* play, Mary-Kate," Lexy said.

"I guess Dana doesn't care about the team," Phoebe said.

Campbell nodded. "Maybe Dana just wanted to get even with Mary-Kate for telling everyone that she took Ashley's forms."

Inside, I felt sick. Everyone still thought Dana had taken my nomination forms. I glanced toward Dana's table.

Dana was sitting with Brooke and Kristen. Everyone else was giving Dana the silent treatment.

If I blabbed about Natalie, though, everyone would start talking about it. The headmistress would find out and cancel the Prom Princess contest. Then it would be *my* fault that the tradition would end—possibly forever.

"There's Mrs. Pritchard. She's going to announce the finalists!" Summer exclaimed.

Phoebe had turned off the camera so she could eat. She picked it up again when Mrs. Pritchard entered. She hit the record button.

Mrs. Pritchard raised her hand for quiet.

All of my friends crossed their fingers for luck—except Phoebe, of course, who needed her fingers to run the camera.

"It's time to announce our two finalists for Prom

Princess," Mrs. Pritchard said. "First, with the most nominations is . . . "

Mary-Kate squeezed my arm.

"Natalie Pittman!" Mrs. Pritchard said, applauding.

"Oh!" Natalie looked surprised. "I can't believe it!"

What a fake! She's not surprised at all, I thought. But I smiled. I was *not* going to be a poor sport.

"Way to go, Natalie!" Rachel stood up and whistled.

"Yea, Natalie!" Tammi yelled.

A bunch of girls cheered. Natalie had gotten a lot of support *without* my signatures. Natalie waved and smiled. *How could Natalie be happy when she cheated to win?* I wondered.

I wanted to win, too. But my being honest was more important.

Mrs. Pritchard waved for quiet. "The second finalist is . . ."

"Please let it be Ashley," Mary-Kate murmured next to me.

"Dana Woletsky!" Mrs. Pritchard applauded again.

"Me?" Dana jumped out of her seat. "This is so cool!"

There was an awkward moment of silence.

"White Oak students are *always* good sports," Mrs. Pritchard said, frowning.

A few girls took the hint and applauded. But no one said a word until the headmistress left.

Then a lot of girls in the dining hall began to whisper and point at Dana. They were upset because they thought Dana had cheated. Nobody wanted her to be a finalist.

Diary, I knew who the cheater was, and it wasn't Dana. I had to do something. But I didn't know what!

Dear Diary,

Dana looked shocked when Mrs. Pritchard called her name. I was shocked, too—I had no idea Dana was such a big faker!

"Dana looked like she didn't *expect* to be one of the finalists," I said to my sister.

"She probably didn't," Ashley whispered in my ear.

"Why not?" I whispered back. "Dana had her signatures and yours. Being a finalist was a sure thing for her."

"It wasn't Dana. I know for a fact that she didn't take my signatures, Mary-Kate," Ashley said.

"What?" I gasped. "I was totally wrong about her?"

"Totally," Ashley whispered. "I'll explain later in private."

Diary, I was stunned! I glanced at Dana again.

"Cheater," Carmen sneered. She was sitting behind Dana. The other girls at her table frowned. Even Brooke and Kristen looked embarrassed to be with Dana.

"But I—" Dana looked around the dining hall with a hurt expression.

Everyone thinks Dana took Ashley's nomination forms, I realized, *because of me.*

Dana has never apologized for the mean things she's done to me. But I had to do the right thing. I stood up. "Dana didn't do anything wrong," I said.

All eyes suddenly turned on me.

"What are you saying, Mary-Kate?" Cheryl asked.

I didn't know what proof Ashley had. But I needed some kind of explanation. "I didn't *see* Dana take Ashley's forms," I said. "The forms probably fell off the clipboard and blew away."

"I bet that's what happened," Ashley added.

Campbell and Phoebe exchanged a puzzled glance.

"I never should have accused you, Dana," I said. "You're a finalist—fair and square." I started to applaud.

55

Ashley stood up and joined in. Then other girls in the dining hall started to applaud. Dana looked relieved.

Ashley leaned closer again. "Come to my room and bring Campbell. I'll tell you what's going on, but it's a secret."

"Okay," I agreed.

Campbell and I hurried to Ashley's room. We perched on the edge of Ashley's bed. Phoebe sat cross-legged on the floor. Ashley turned her desk chair to face us and sat down.

"Okay, Ashley," Phoebe said. "What's going on?"

"I got called to Mrs. Pritchard's office today." Ashley took a deep breath. "And so did Natalie."

"Why?" I asked.

"The same eight girls signed forms for both of us," Ashley said.

It took me a moment to understand what that meant.

"Eight!" Phoebe gasped. "That's how many girls signed for you a second time, Ashley. After your forms were lost."

My eyes got wide. "The same eight girls' names were on your form and Natalie's because *Natalie* was using your original forms!"

"Yep," Ashley said.

"Oh, no!" I slapped my hand to my forehead. "I

remember now! Natalie was looking over my shoulder when I pulled a new form out of your clipboard."

"When the other forms fell out?" Ashley asked.

I nodded. "Natalie dropped her clipboard at the same time. Her papers fell off. I probably figured all the pages were hers."

"That was right when we were all called onto the field, wasn't it?" Campbell said.

I nodded. "So I was distracted. And Natalie must have picked up your forms when she picked up hers, Ashley."

"On purpose or by accident?" Phoebe asked.

"That doesn't matter now," I said. "Natalie *knew* she had Ashley's missing forms when she handed them in. All the contestants know exactly how many signatures they had *and* who signed their forms."

"So Dana is innocent," Campbell said. "And Natalie is a cheat."

"*And* a finalist," I pointed out.

"We can't let Natalie get away with this," Phoebe said. Her eyes flashed. "We've got to tell Mrs. Pritchard."

"We can't," Ashley said. "Nobody can tell *anyone*."

"Why not?" Campbell asked.

"If Mrs. Pritchard finds out that someone cheated," Ashley explained, "she'll cancel the Prom Princess contest. There might not be another one—ever."

"I don't want *that* to be our fault!" Campbell exclaimed.

"Neither do I," Phoebe said. "Besides, then Ashley and I won't have a movie project."

"But we can't let Natalie off the hook," I said.

"I agree, but we have to handle this ourselves," Ashley insisted. "No teachers or anything."

"Okay," Campbell said. "How?"

"I have an idea," Ashley said. "Natalie cheated to be the Prom Princess. So let's make sure she *doesn't* win."

"I love it!" Phoebe exclaimed.

"So do I," Campbell said. "It's the *perfect* payback."

"But how can we make sure Natalie doesn't get the most votes at the Spring Prom?" I asked.

"We'll make sure that *Dana* does," Ashley said.

My mouth fell open. "Are you crazy?"

Ashley shook her head. "It's the only way, Mary-Kate."

So that's where things stand, Diary. I'm going to help my worst enemy, Dana Woletsky, win the Prom Princess contest!

Chapter 8

Tuesday

Dear Diary,

Phoebe, Mary-Kate, Campbell, and I stayed in my room until curfew. We came up with a plan to help Dana win the Prom Princess contest *and* save our video. Getting Dana to star in our video was only Phase One.

"What if Dana doesn't want to be in our video?" Phoebe asked the next morning.

"We can't take no for an answer," I said, "or we won't have a video at all."

"Right," Phoebe agreed, picking up the camera. "Do you think Dana can get more votes than Natalie at the dance?"

"Sure," I said. Getting more girls to vote for Dana was Phase Two. "Dana is one of the most popular girls in school."

"Even if she *is* bossy and a snob," Phoebe added with a grin. "At least she isn't a *cheat* like Natalie."

"Let's see what Summer and Elise found out," I said. My friends had agreed to ask other girls who they were going to vote for: Natalie or Dana.

Phoebe followed me out of our room and downstairs to the lounge. Summer and Elise were waiting for us on the sofa.

"Ashley, Phoebe," Elise said, waving us over.

"What did you guys find out?" I asked.

Phoebe stood back with the camera. I had told her to tape everything from now on. We didn't know which scenes would make our video more interesting.

"Half the girls we talked to are going to vote for Natalie," Elise said. "They think she's nicer than Dana and deserves it more."

I knew that wasn't true, but I couldn't say anything.

"Dana has the 'in crowd' vote tied up," Summer said.

I wasn't surprised to hear that. All the snobby girls stuck together.

"But the final Prom Princess vote will be by secret ballot," Elise added. "So things might change. If some girls don't have to worry that Dana will be mad at them, they might vote for Natalie instead of her."

The news wasn't great. It was going to be a very close race.

Phoebe put the camera on pause and followed me outside. "Kristen told me that Dana is at the *Acorn* working on her softball article."

"Let's go talk to her," I said as we headed across campus.

Prom Princess

The *Acorn* office was crowded. The next edition of the paper was due out on Saturday.

One girl was looking through a stack of photos. Another girl was typing at a computer. Ms. Bloomberg, the faculty adviser for the newspaper, was reading student articles. Taylor and Ellen were filming the teacher for their video project.

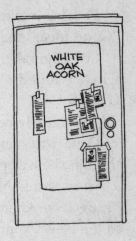

"There's Dana," I said, pointing. Dana was sitting at a desk in the corner. We walked over.

"What do you want, Ashley?" Dana asked, looking up. She frowned at Phoebe. "Turn the camera off."

"I'm making a video about the Prom Princess contest, Dana," I said. "You're a finalist, so I'd like an interview."

"I'm too busy for your little video," Dana said.

I bit my lip. I wasn't sure if she was really busy or still mad at Mary-Kate——and taking it out on me!

Phoebe looked at me. I could see she was trying to figure out what to do. I got an idea. "Well, that's too bad," I said. "I know, Phoebe, maybe Natalie will do it. I'm sure that starring in a video might help her get some extra Prom Princess votes."

Phoebe looked shocked. Then she caught on. "Good idea," she said.

"We should do everything we can to help her win," I added. "We don't want to make a video about a loser."

"Absolutely not," Phoebe agreed.

Dana was hanging on to every word now, even though she was pretending to ignore us.

"I'm sure Natalie will sign on," I said. "Especially when she finds out this video might be in the New Hampshire Film Festival."

Now Dana looked up. "Seriously?" she said. "A real film festival? With movie stars and everything?"

I smiled. "That's the one."

"All right," Dana agreed. "I'll do it."

I grinned. "Great!"

Phase One was now complete.

Dear Diary,

I went to softball practice today even though I couldn't play. I wanted to show my support for the team.

There was another reason I was there: I promised Ashley that I would help Dana win the Prom Princess contest. So I was going to try to convince my softball friends to vote for Dana instead of Natalie.

I know, Diary. I'm not thrilled about helping the

one person at White Oak who seems to have it in for me. Life can really get strange.

Just as I expected, Dana was sitting in the bleachers taking notes for her article.

"Hi, Dana." I sat down beside her.

"What are you doing here?" Dana asked with a frown.

"I came to watch practice," I said, already annoyed. Then I reminded myself of Ashley's goal.

"I also wanted to apologize again," I said. I still felt bad for calling Dana a thief.

"Okay," Dana said. There was a long pause. Then she asked, "How's your arm?"

"Fine," I said, moving my arm around. "Not even a cramp."

"Good," Dana said. She turned to watch the field. I did, too.

Mindy was playing first base instead of me. That hurt, but I didn't let it show.

Brandy Oliver struck out. Campbell hit a pop fly into the outfield, but Caitlin missed it. Campbell was safe on first.

"You're supposed to catch it, Caitlin!" Dana shouted. "That should have been an easy out!"

I knew that Caitlin would probably vote for

Dana. But that could change if Dana was mean to her. "Come on, Dana," I said. "This is just practice, not a game."

"Good thing," Dana said, rolling her eyes.

Natalie came up to bat next. She slammed a drive down the first base line, but Mindy wasn't paying attention. The ball whizzed right by her. Natalie ran to third, and Campbell crossed home plate.

"Wake up, Mindy!" Dana yelled. She shook her head and wrote something in her notebook.

"Are you writing about Caitlin's and Mindy's mistakes for your article, Dana?" I asked.

"A good reporter has to report the facts," Dana said. "It's not like I'm making it up."

"No, but the team practices so we don't make the same mistakes during a game," I explained. "Besides, I wouldn't want you to lose Caitlin's and Mindy's votes for Prom Princess."

"Since when do you care, Mary-Kate?" Dana snapped.

I couldn't tell Dana that Ashley and I wanted to help her win so that Natalie wouldn't. I shrugged. "I just do, okay? So why not write good things about the team?"

"Because I want the Mighty Oaks to *win*," Dana said. "Mount Truman won the Conference Championship last year. They'll be a tough team to beat."

I was shocked. "If you're so worried about winning this Friday, why did you rat me out to Coach Hadley?" I asked.

"Because I want the Mighty Oaks to win the Conference Championship this year," Dana said. "That means *you* have to play the *other* eleven games this season."

"Huh?" I frowned, confused.

"You're one of the best hitters on the team, Mary-Kate," Dana said.

I was stunned to hear Dana admit that I was a good player.

"If you try to hit homers before your arm is okay," Dana went on, "you could be out for the whole season. Then White Oak might lose."

"But I might not be able to break Jamie Jerome's home-run record if I don't play on Friday," I blurted.

"What's more important to you, Mary-Kate— a championship for the whole team or a record for yourself?" Dana asked.

I didn't say anything, Diary, but I knew she was right: the team comes first.

I just didn't like hearing that from Dana!

Chapter 9

Thursday

Dear Diary,

Okay, Diary, tell me: why are people so difficult?

Dana wants my video to be the White Oak entry in the Film Festival so she that can be a star, right? So I thought she might be a little less snotty and a lot more cooperative than usual. That's a joke—on me! The problems started at breakfast.

Phoebe was taping Dana as she carried her tray to a table. As soon as she sat down, Dana made a chopping gesture with her hand. "Cut!" Dana ordered. "Turn the camera off!"

"What's the problem, Dana?" I asked.

"She's taping my left side," Dana said. "My *right* side is my best profile."

"Move to her right side, Phoebe," I said.

"Now *I* won't be in the picture," Brooke complained. She was sitting on Dana's right, behind Phoebe.

Kirsten, Brooke, and Lisa all wanted to be in our video, now that Dana was the star.

"Pan the camera around the table so everyone gets in, Phoebe," I said. "Okay, everyone, just act natural."

Boy, was *that* a mistake, Diary! I shouldn't have

said anything. Everyone started acting like robots!

"What—are—you—wearing—to—the—dance?" Kristen asked Dana. She paused between every word.

"A dress," Dana answered. She dipped her spoon into her oatmeal.

"Whatcolorisit?" Brooke asked. She ran all her words together.

"Gold," Dana said. "It totally rocks. Of course." She smirked. "Nobody here has the great taste that I do. I always dress better than everyone else."

"Cut!" I exclaimed. I couldn't use a scene with Dana insulting the clothing choices of the entire student body! "Phoebe and I have got to eat, too. See you later, Dana."

"But I haven't told you about my shoes," Dana protested.

"Later," Phoebe said, turning off the camera. "I'm starving." We went to sit with our friends at another table.

After breakfast, Phoebe and I followed Dana down the hall to our first class.

"What do you want me to do, Ashley?" Dana asked.

A documentary is a record of real people and events. I didn't want my video to look fake. "Just do what you usually do," I said.

We passed Holly Welsh and Jolene Dupree by the drinking fountain. They were talking about the Spring Prom.

"I'm wearing my hair up in these cute little glitter clips," Jolene was saying. "How are you wearing your hair?"

Holly shrugged. "The way I always do," she said. Her straight dark, hair was pulled back tightly and tied at the base of her neck.

Dana stopped. "You've *got* to do something different with your hair, Holly."

"B-but I always wear it like this," Holly said.

Dana raised an eyebrow. It was clear she didn't like Holly's hairstyle. "You should cut it short and curl it. That would soften your angular face."

"My what?" Holly looked upset. Something told me that she wasn't going to vote for Dana.

"No need to thank me." Dana smiled at her and moved on.

Phoebe skipped to get ahead of Dana. We wanted lots of different shots for the video.

"You know what, Phoebe? You should wear contacts," Dana said. "No one can see what color your eyes are behind your glasses."

Phoebe frowned. I could tell she wasn't sure if Dana had just insulted her or not.

I flipped open my notebook and made a note: *Holly, hair; Phoebe, glasses: Is Dana being mean, or is she trying to help?*

Later, at lunch, Phoebe, Dana, and I sat with Layne and Carmen. They had nominated Lavender, but she wasn't a finalist. I hoped we could convince them to vote for Dana.

As usual, Phoebe had the camera ready and running when we started talking about the Spring Prom.

"Who are you going to the dance with, Dana?" Layne asked.

"Brent Lowell and Eric Mason both asked me," Dana said. "I decided to go with Brent."

"How could you decide?" Carmen asked. "They are both really cute guys."

"Brent's taller," Dana said. "I don't think the Prom Prince should be shorter than the Prom Princess, do you?"

"I guess not," Layne answered.

"She means *if* she wins the contest," I added. Dana didn't seem to know that it was annoying when she sounded too confident.

"Who are you going to the dance with, Carmen?" Dana asked.

"I don't have a date," Carmen said.

"That's okay." Dana shrugged. "Nobody will say anything if you go to the Spring Prom alone—not to your face, anyway."

Carmen looked startled.

Dana really doesn't know that she just insulted Carmen, I realized. *That's probably another vote for Natalie.*

"I'm taking my camera to the prom," Phoebe said to break the tension. "But it's not a very good dancer."

Everyone laughed.

We had biology class after lunch. Blair was in the corner filming her green bean video.

"You're doing a movie about *this* bean plant, Blair?" Dana asked. She pointed to the potted plant on the windowsill. "It's wilted."

"No, it isn't," Blair said. She sounded annoyed. "I'm sure it's fine."

Actually, Dana was right. The bean plant looked limp.

"It's not fine," Dana said. "My grandmother's house is full of plants. I've learned a lot from her. You should repot this sad thing in dry soil. And hold the water for a day or two."

Blair scowled as Dana moved to her seat.

I'm positive Dana tries to help, Diary. It just doesn't seem like it most of the time.

For a popular girl, Dana sure knows how to get people mad at her! And it could cost her the Prom Princess contest!

Dear Diary,

I sat in the backstage lounge of the auditorium waiting for Dana. It was Ashley's idea, in case Dana needed anything before she made her speech.

I didn't think Dana would want me around for anything, but if that's what my sister wanted, fine.

When Natalie came into the lounge, I pulled out my notebook. I acted like I was studying. Otherwise, it would be too hard to pretend I didn't know she had stolen Ashley's forms.

Dana came in a few minutes later. She was wearing low-rise brown corduroys, a tan pullover sweater, and brown shoes with a low heel. The outfit gave her a serious-student-with-style look.

I walked over to Dana. "Are you all set?" I asked.

"Yeah." Dana nodded. She glanced at the note cards she was carrying. "I hope my speech isn't too long. We're not supposed to talk for more than three minutes."

"I could time your speech, if you want," I offered.

"Great!" Dana said. She glanced over at Natalie. "Let's find someplace private."

I followed Dana to the area behind the stage curtain. No one would bother us there.

I looked at my watch and waited a couple of seconds. Then I gave her the signal to start. "Right . . . now."

"Only one Prom Princess is chosen every year at White Oak," Dana began. "She's always someone who stands out from the crowd, a leader among students. There is no doubt about it—that someone is me! Who else could she possibly be?"

I rocked back in surprise. A White Oak Prom Princess definitely didn't brag!

What am I going to do? I wondered as Dana kept talking. *If Dana gives this speech, she'll lose the contest for sure.*

"Well?" Dana asked when she finished.

I glanced at my watch. "The timing is perfect, but . . ." How could I tell Dana to change her speech without getting her really mad? "You . . . uh . . . probably shouldn't say that you set *all* the trends at White Oak."

"But I do!" Dana exclaimed. "I get all the latest styles first. That's how everyone here knows what to wear."

"I know that," I said. "But so does everyone else."

"Oh, yeah." Dana nodded. "I see what you mean."

"And," I went on, "pointing out that some girls beg to sit at your table probably won't be a big vote-getter."

"Why not?" Dana asked, puzzled. "Lots of girls ask to sit with me in the dining hall."

"How many do you turn down?" I asked.

"Most of them," Dana said. Then her eyes widened. "Would they hold that against me?"

"Maybe," I said. "So why remind them?"

"Whatever." Dana looked annoyed. "Anything else?"

"Well, maybe we could make your speech about what the perfect Prom Princess should be," I said. "And just *hint* that you're the best choice."

"I don't have time to write a new speech!" Dana protested.

I remembered something Dana had said to me at softball practice. "I've got an idea," I said. "Come on!"

I knew the drama teacher kept a clipboard and pen in the prop room. I pushed open the door and stepped into the dark room. I knew it was full of sets, wardrobe racks, and boxes of props.

"Watch your step," I warned Dana, but it was too late.

"Ouch!" Dana cried out. "I tripped over something."

I found the light switch and flipped on the light.

"Oh, no!" Dana squealed. "I broke the heel off my shoe!"

"You can wear mine," I said. Dana glanced at me and wrinkled her nose. I was wearing a Mighty Oaks sweatshirt, jeans, and black sneakers. Not exactly Dana's style.

"I'd rather limp on one heel," Dana said.

"Check the wardrobe boxes," I suggested.

I reached for the clipboard on the wall. The pen was attached to it with a string. I sat on the floor and turned the note cards over to write on the blank side while Dana searched through boxes.

"This box is marked 'shoes'!" Dana said. She leaned over an upside-down bicycle to reach the boxes. "Maybe there will be something in here."

"I hope so," I said. I kept writing as Dana tried on a pair of black flats.

"They're too small," Dana complained.

I looked up and gasped. Dana's sweater was streaked with black grime from the bicycle.

Prom Princess

Dana looked down at the black mark. She threw up her hands. "Now what am I going to do?"

Just then, I heard the sound of applause. Mrs. Pritchard's voice came over the loudspeakers. "Good evening, young ladies. I know you're all eager to hear from our Prom Princess finalists. We'll begin with Natalie Pittman."

"We have to do something!" Dana said. "I'm up in three minutes!"

"Don't panic, Dana!" I said.

I crossed my fingers behind my back and wished for luck. Because, Diary, we really needed it!

Chapter 10

Thursday

Dear Diary,

Phoebe and I had front-row, center seats so we could tape the Prom Princess speeches.

"Showtime," Phoebe said when Natalie walked onto the stage.

"I am absolutely *thrilled* to be a Prom Princess finalist," Natalie said. She was wearing a cranberry-red skirt with a matching sweater over a T-shirt. "And so surprised!" she added.

"Sure she is," I said under my breath.

"In fact," Natalie went on, "being nominated for Prom Princess is one of the best things that's ever happened to me. It's even more exciting than when I won the school spelling bee, or that gold medal I got at the championship swim meet."

I rolled my eyes.

"But then the ideal White Oak student tries to be the best at everything she does," Natalie went on. "I know I do."

You cheat to win, Natalie! I thought. No one in the audience knew that, or seemed to care that Natalie was bragging.

"Success is built on hard work, determination, and a winning attitude," Natalie said. "For me, being Prom Princess will be a dream come true. So I'd like your vote at the Spring Prom."

The crowd applauded as Natalie left the stage.

"And now, Dana," Phoebe said. She refocused her camera.

Dana stepped onto the stage—and I couldn't believe my eyes, Diary! Dana, who always looks as if she stepped out of a fashion magazine, was wearing brown pants with Mary-Kate's sweatshirt and black sneakers.

Several girls in the audience giggled as Dana walked to center stage. Dana just looked over the crowd and smiled. "Being Prom Princess is a thrill for every girl who has ever been chosen," Dana said. "But the crown does not belong to the winners alone."

"It doesn't?" Phoebe asked in a whisper.

I shrugged, but Dana had my attention!

"Every Prom Princess shares the honor with the girls who voted for her," Dana went on. "She wouldn't be Prom Princess without the support of her friends and fellow students. We're all a team at White Oak."

Dana struck a cheerleader's pose with her hands on her hips and her feet apart. Then she pointed to

 the Mighty Oaks logo on her sweatshirt. "Just like the Mighty Oaks!" she declared.

Someone in the crowd whistled. Others cheered.

"So I'm asking for your vote at the dance on Saturday," Dana said with a huge grin. "And don't forget to come to the Mighty Oaks' softball game tomorrow afternoon!"

Dana led the crowd in a White Oak cheer. She ended by yelling, "Go, Oaks!" Then she ran off the stage. Everyone applauded wildly.

"That was fantastic!" Phoebe's smile was almost as big as mine. Dana's speech was inspired!

My good feeling about Dana's chances of winning the Prom Princess contest lasted all night. I didn't have *any* doubts—until Phoebe and I started to edit our movie Friday afternoon.

We were in the Young Filmmakers Club meeting room. We finally had a title: *The Making of a Prom Princess*. But we were having trouble finding video that we could use.

I shook my head. "We need ten minutes of video when Dana isn't being bossy, rude, or stuck-up."

"Everybody loved Dana's speech," Phoebe said.

"That's only three minutes," I pointed out. "We can't have seven minutes of Dana being . . . Dana."

"Probably not," Phoebe agreed. "But Dana isn't always as mean as she sounds."

"We know that, but how many other girls do?" I asked.

"Does Dana have *any* chance to win Prom Princess?" Phoebe asked.

"I don't know," I said. "I just don't know."

Dear Diary,

I sat on the bench while the Mighty Oaks warmed up for the game against Mount Truman. Classes were over for the week, and everyone had turned out to cheer the team on.

Dana came into the dugout with her notebook. Her report about the game would be in tomorrow's issue of the *Acorn*.

"Hi, Dana," I said. "From what I hear, everyone thought your speech was fantastic."

"I know. Thanks," Dana said. "Did the nurse check your arm this morning?"

"Yes, it's completely healed," I said. I didn't mention that I was still benched for disobeying Coach's order not to practice—thanks to Dana!

"Well, that's good," Dana said. She sat down and

opened her notebook. I turned my attention to the game.

In the first inning, a Mount Truman batter hit a high fly between first and second. Natalie was playing first base for the Mighty Oaks. The batter ran past first toward second. But Natalie left first base, too.

"Should Natalie be going for that ball?" Dana asked me.

"Not really," I said. Lexy ran in from the outfield to make the catch. Natalie caught the ball instead.

"Well, at least Natalie got the out," Dana said.

I watched as the runner going for second turned and ran safely back to first.

"But if Natalie had stayed on first, Lexy would have thrown to her," I explained. "Natalie could have tagged the runner out. Then we'd have *two* outs."

The Mount Truman team was still two runs ahead in the fourth inning. There was no one on base for White Oak when Natalie stepped up to bat.

"If Natalie can just get on base, we might tie the score this inning," I said.

"I hope you're right, Mary-Kate," Dana said.

Natalie hit a hard drive to center field. We all cheered her to keep going when she rounded first base.

"Watch out, Natalie!" I screamed when Natalie

touched second and headed for third. The Mount Truman outfielder had her arm drawn back to throw the ball.

"Stay there!" Dana shouted when Natalie made it to third.

But Natalie raced for home. The outfielder threw to the catcher. The catcher caught the ball and tagged Natalie out before she crossed home plate.

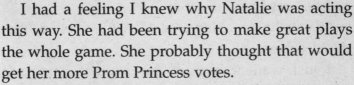

All the Mighty Oaks in the dugout groaned.

"Why did Natalie do that?" Dana was furious. "She was safe at third!"

I had a feeling I knew why Natalie was acting this way. She had been trying to make great plays the whole game. She probably thought that would get her more Prom Princess votes.

"I wish I could be on the field helping the team," I said, mostly to myself. Dana stared at me, then smiled. I have no idea why. Mount Truman was still ahead by two runs when the Mighty Oaks got up to bat in the last inning. The team needed three runs to win.

Dana suddenly left the dugout and talked to Coach Hadley for a few minutes. Then she sat in the bleachers with her friends.

Samantha Kramer struck out, and Kayla Bailey was tagged out at first. Lexy and Campbell both hit singles. They were on first and second with two outs when Natalie got up to bat.

Coach Hadley stopped Natalie from leaving the dugout. "Sit down, Natalie. You've been playing to make yourself look good all afternoon. We need a team player to bat for us now."

"But I—" Natalie stopped herself and sat down, frowning.

"Okay, Mary-Kate," Coach Hadley said. "You're up."

"Me?" I was surprised, but I didn't ask questions. I quickly put on the batting helmet and grabbed my bat.

"Get a homer, Mary-Kate!" Ashley yelled from the bleachers.

I just wanted a good hit so that Lexy and Campbell could score. Helping the team win was more important than my own home-run glory.

"Come on, Mary-Kate!" someone else yelled. "You can do it."

I looked up. I couldn't tell who had shouted, but Dana was giving me a thumbs-up!

Did Dana ask the coach to let me play? I wondered.

I gripped the bat. The first pitch was right across the plate. I swung and slammed the bat against the ball. It sailed toward the outfield, and I raced for first.

"It's going!" someone shouted.

"Going, going, gone!" The crowd cheered.

A home run! I saw the ball disappear over the fence. Lexy and Campbell scored as I ran the bases.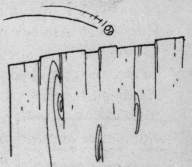

"Mary-Kate! Mary-Kate!" everyone chanted.

I crossed home plate to score the winning run.

White Oak had won the first game of the season!

And I had my first homer toward breaking Jamie Jerome's record.

I know I said that I hoped Dana wouldn't win the Prom Princess contest, Diary. Well, I've changed my mind.

Chapter 11

Saturday

Dear Diary,

First thing in the morning, someone pounded on my door. "Open up, Mary-Kate!" Ashley called.

Campbell was stretched out on her bed, so I jumped out of my bed to open the door. Ashley and Phoebe rushed in.

"Look at this!" Ashley pulled a copy of the *Acorn* out of her backpack and held it up.

The headline read: "Mighty Oaks Win!" Right below that, it read: "Mary-Kate on Track to Break Home-run Record!"

I took the paper from Ashley and read the article. Dana had written about all the highlights of the game. She even praised all the players for trying hard and not giving up. She did not mention that Coach Hadley had taken Natalie out of the game.

I read the last sentence aloud: "'Mary-Kate Burke has a good chance of breaking Jamie Jerome's home-run record while she's still in First Form.'"

"It's hard to believe Dana wrote that," Campbell said.

"Well, Dana isn't always as mean and nasty as everyone thinks," Ashley said. "Not all the time, anyway."

Phoebe grinned. "We've got some great examples on video of Dana being brutally nice."

I couldn't imagine that Dana and I would ever be close friends. I was just happy she wasn't giving me a hard time!

And, Diary, guess what? I was even happy that I was going to vote for her!

Dear Diary,

What a day! Phoebe and I hung "Vote for Dana" posters all over campus. Some of our friends handed out flyers for her. Then we went to tape Dana getting ready for the Prom.

"I'm going to pull your hair up and back into a twist," Brooke said. "It will look elegant, and the princess tiara will fit right over it."

"*If* I win," Dana corrected.

I was totally shocked. Dana actually admitted that *not* winning was a very big possibility!

"I heard some girls on

the softball team talking this morning," Kristen said.

"Did they like my article in the *Acorn*?" Dana asked.

"Loved it," Kristen said. "And they're upset with Natalie for almost costing them the game yesterday."

"So they're going to vote for you, Dana," Brooke said.

"Fantastic!" I said.

"Yeah," Kristen agreed. "It's still going to be close."

"I don't want to talk about it," Dana snapped. She looked at Phoebe. "No more camera, okay? Come back at seven o'clock when I'm ready to leave."

"Okay," I said. "Phoebe and I have to get dressed, too. Brent won't mind being on camera, will he?"

Brent was Dana's date. He would be waiting in the Student Union with all the boys from Harrington.

"No way," Dana said. "He's a big ham."

Mary-Kate and Campbell came to my room just as Phoebe and I finished dressing.

"Wow!" Mary-Kate exclaimed. "You guys look gorgeous!"

"Thanks!" My dress was lavender. Phoebe had braided a sprig of tiny purple flowers with purple and white ribbons into my hair. "So do you!"

Mary-Kate's dress was pale pink with sparkly straps. She wore her hair high on her head.

Campbell wore a dark green skirt with a light green top. Phoebe had found a light blue 1950s dress at a thrift shop. It was tied with a huge bow in the back.

We all went over to Phipps House to pick up Dana. Kristen and Brooke were waiting with her in the lounge. Phoebe had the camera going when Dana made her grand entrance into the Student Union. Brent was waiting for her.

"You look great, Dana!" Brent grinned.

"Thanks. Will you get me some soda, Brent?" Dana asked. "I'm so nervous, my throat is dry."

I gestured for Phoebe to pan the room. The prom theme was "Spring Garden." The whole hall was decorated with flowers, greenery, fluffy fake animals, and white picket fences. Cotton clouds were hanging from the ceiling on strings. A D.J. was set up on a stage at the far end of the room.

"I see Ross and Jordan," Mary-Kate said. She nodded to our boyfriends, who were standing by the snack table.

"I already told Ross I'd be busy with my video

the first part of dance," I explained. "Will you and Jordan hang out with him until after the Prom Princess is announced?"

"No problem," Mary-Kate said. She hurried off to join her date—and mine!

Dana sat down at a table and stared nervously at the ballot box.

The large box was decorated with flowers, streamers, and birds. A teacher handed out ballots and checked off names to make sure no one voted more than one time.

"Get some shots of people voting, Phoebe," I directed.

"I'm on it," Phoebe said. She aimed the camera at the line of girls in front of the ballot box. She panned back to Dana's table when Blair came up.

"Thank you, Dana," Blair said. "I repotted my plant. It perked up just enough for me to get some great shots before I picked the beans."

"That's nice." Dana kept watching the ballot box.

"Wow! Look at Holly!" Phoebe trained the camera on the girl and pointed with her free hand.

I looked over. Holly was waiting in line to vote. She had taken Dana's advice, too. Her hair was short and curly. The new style *did* soften her angular face.

Holly waved her ballot when she caught my eye. *Is she voting for Dana?* I wondered.

Brent came back to Dana's table with a soda. "Come on, Dana, let's dance," he suggested.

"Good idea!" I nodded. Our video of the dance would be hopelessly dull if Dana just stared at the ballot box all night. "It'll help pass the time."

Phoebe and I caught everything on camera. We even got a shot of the teacher taking the ballot box away to count the votes.

Then—*finally*—Mrs. Pritchard walked out on stage to announce the winner of the Prom Princess contest.

I was as nervous as Dana! Would our video project be called *The Making of a Prom Princess: Winner* or *The Making of a Prom Princess: Loser*?

Chapter 12

Saturday

Dear Diary,

I rushed over to Ashley when Mrs. Pritchard walked onto the stage. Campbell, Jordan, and Ross came with me. "I can't stand the suspense!" I said.

"Dana's going to win," Campbell said. "I feel it."

"I *so* hope that's true!" Ashley grinned.

Phoebe aimed the camera at the stage.

"I'd like to welcome you all to White Oak's Spring Prom," Mrs. Pritchard said. "I'm sure you're all anxious to know who this year's Prom Princess is, but first—"

A groan went through the crowd.

Dana gripped Brent's hand. Kristen and Brooke stood close behind her. Natalie smiled with her hands tightly clasped.

"Let's have a round of applause for the decorating committee!" Mrs. Pritchard clapped her hands.

The crowd's applause was polite and ended quickly. Everyone wanted to know who had won the contest!

"I'd like to thank all the teachers who helped make the Spring Prom a fabulous success," Mrs. Pritchard said. "Even the voting went smoothly."

The D.J. stepped up beside the headmistress.

"And I think everyone would *really* like to know who won," he said.

"Nobody cares about *that*, do they?" Mrs. Pritchard joked. "All right. I'm happy to announce that the winner of White Oak's First Form Prom Princess contest is—"

Ashley grabbed my arm and squeezed.

"Dana Woletsky!" Mrs. Pritchard said.

Dana screamed in total surprise. Kristen and Brooke jumped up and down, squealing.

"Yes!" I yelled. I whistled and cheered and gave Ashley a high five. "We did it, Ashley! We did it!"

Ashley hugged me. "Thanks for helping."

Phoebe was excited, too, but she was still taping. She was trying not to jiggle the camera!

Brent took Dana's hand and led her onto the stage.

I looked at Natalie. She wasn't smiling anymore. She ran out of the hall in tears.

"It's too bad you weren't in the Prom Princess finals, Ashley," I said. "But at least you got a happy ending."

Ashley nodded. "And I sort of made friends with Dana."

"Me too," I said, much to my own surprise.

"I'm pleased to crown Dana the Princess of the Spring Prom!" Mrs. Pritchard placed a sparkling

rhinestone tiara on Dana's head. "Would you like to say a few words or thank anyone, Dana?"

"Get ready to take a bow, Ashley," Phoebe said. She looked up from the camera.

Ashley smiled and motioned for Phoebe to keep filming.

"This is so fantastic!" Dana gushed with a huge smile. "I want to thank my best friends, Kristen and Brooke, for sticking by me even though they didn't nominate me."

Kristen and Brooke took quick, embarrassed bows.

"And Mrs. Pritchard and the teachers who made the Spring Prom and the Prom Princess contest possible," Dana went on.

Mrs. Pritchard beamed. "Thank you, Dana."

"And last but not least," Dana said, "you should be very glad you voted for me. I worked really hard and totally deserve this!"

Dana took Brent's hand, and they stepped off the stage. They started to dance when the D.J. cued up a slow song.

"What?" Phoebe exclaimed. "That's it? What about thanking you two?"

Ashley and I broke out laughing.

"Oh, well," Ashley said. "She's still the same old self-centered Dana."

"Yeah." I giggled. "Some things never change."

Dear Diary,

Ashley came to my room after the last meeting of the Young Filmmakers Club today. She sat on my bed while I changed out of my softball uniform.

"How did the game go, Mary-Kate?" Ashley asked.

"We beat Bradenton," I said. "Six to three." I grinned. "And I hit a home run! My second for the season—with ten games to go."

"That is fantastic!" Ashley exclaimed.

"Thanks. How did things go with your movie?" I asked.

"Okay, I guess," Ashley answered. "*The Making of a Prom Princess* was voted the *second*-best video."

"Second?" I gasped. "That means your video won't be in the film festival."

"No." Ashley shook her head. "Blair's movie was chosen for the White Oak entry in the student category."

I blinked. "Your Prom Princess video got beaten by *The Life and Death of a Green Bean*?"

Ashley shrugged. "That's showbiz."

I shook my head. "Dana won't be happy. She wanted to be discovered by Hollywood at the film festival. Now she's been bested by a green bean!"

"It's worse than that!" Ashley said. "Dana was beaten by a green bean that *she* saved with some brutally good gardening advice!"

That sent both of us into howls of laughter.

Dear Diary,

"Listen up, Teen Spirit," I said, down at the lake after lunch. "It's time we talked about what our band's going to wear. Music isn't just about music anymore—it's about image!"

Phoebe put down her guitar and jumped up. "What if we wear all black?" she asked. "Maybe black velvet with lots and lots of silver jewelry!"

"Nice!" I agreed.

Erin groaned. "Only if you're in an orchestra."

Phoebe frowned. "What do you mean by that?"

Erin stood up. "When I think of our rock 'n' roll band, I think eye-popping color. I think . . . pink!"

"Pink?" Phoebe repeated.

"I think everything we wear should be pink," Erin

explained. "Pink tees, pink pants, flip-flops—"

I smiled as I pictured the band all pinked-out. I love the color pink! I held up my hand to high-five Erin.

"What do you think, Phoebe?" I asked.

Phoebe stared at me long and hard. She finally blinked and said, "You've got to be kidding."

"Here we go again." Erin sighed.

"We're a band—not cartoon characters!" Phoebe said. "The only pink outfit I own is a coat from the 1950s with a matching veiled hat. And that's back home in San Francisco!"

"I'm sorry you don't like my idea, Phoebe," Erin said. "But Ashley does, so I guess you're outnumbered."

Phoebe shot me a look. "Ashley?" she asked.

My stomach flip-flopped. I was in the middle again!

"Um," I told Erin. "Maybe we can wear Phoebe's silver jewelry with the outfits?" I smiled at Phoebe.

"As long as the jewelry has pink beads," Erin said.

Phoebe groaned. She picked up her guitar and huffed away.

Diary, can I help it if I like Erin's ideas more than Phoebe's? But now I feel totally trapped between my old friend and my new friend. What am I going to do?

Dear Diary,

Here's the scoop: Janelle and I are in the same band. So is Lark, which is why I'm kind of bummed out.

It all started when we met our instructor, Bill.

"Bill?" I said, glancing at Lark. "Can our band have two singers? I want to sing. And I think Lark does, too."

"Really?" Bill said. He ignored me and smiled at Lark. "Do you, Lark? Do you want to sing?"

"Sure," Lark said with a shrug. She didn't look very excited. But then again, she never did.

"Then we'll both sing, right?" I asked Bill.

"Sorry, Mary-Kate," Bill said. "But every band has only one lead singer."

Am I missing something? I wondered. Lark didn't even sing at last night's campfire. And now she's going to sing lead?

"Bill?" I asked in a low voice. "May I speak to you, please? In private?"

"Sure thing," Bill said, still smiling at Lark.

The two of us walked over to a nearby tree. I spoke in a low voice. "I was kind of hoping I'd get to sing," I said. "I was the star of my school musicals. Can't Lark play an instrument?" I asked. We all had to write one down on the Camp Rock 'n' Roll application.

"It's cool," Bill said. "We'll just give Lark a tambourine she can shake around."

I was really confused now! What was all the fuss about Lark?

"Speaking of instruments, Mary-Kate," Bill said. "You wrote on your application that you play piano. Check?"

My eyes flew wide open. Piano? I took my last piano lesson when I was ten years old!

"I did take lessons," I said slowly.

"Great!" Bill said. "We'll get you a keyboard tomorrow, and you can start jamming. If you play piano, you'll be able to ace the keyboard in no time."

"C-c-cool!" I stammered.

But it really wasn't.

I still wanted to sing lead. And how could I tell Bill that the only song I learned to play on the piano was "The Itsy Bitsy Spider"?

Mary-Kate And Ashley *NEW YORK MINUTE*
"Win Free Tickets" Sweepstakes

OFFICIAL RULES:

1. NO PURCHASE OR PAYMENT NECESSARY.

2. **How to Enter.** To enter, complete the official entry form or hand print your name, address, age, and phone number along with
   words "New York Minute Win Free Tickets Sweepstakes" on a 3" x 5" card and mail to: New York Minute Win Free Tic
   Sweepstakes, c/o HarperEntertainment, Attn: Children's Marketing Department, 10 East 53rd Street, New York, NY 10022. En
   must be received no later than **April 30, 2004.** Enter as often as you wish, but each entry must be mailed separately. One e
   per envelope. Partially completed, illegible, or mechanically reproduced entries will not be accepted. Sponsors are not responsible
   lost, late, mutilated, illegible, stolen, postage due, incomplete, or misdirected entries. All entries become the property of Dua
   Entertainment Group, LLC, and will not be returned.

3. **Eligibility.** Sweepstakes open to all legal residents of the United States, (excluding Colorado and Rhode Island), who are betw
   the ages of five and fifteen on **May 1, 2004,** excluding employees and immediate family members of HarperCollins Publishers,
   ("HarperCollins"), Warner Bros. Pictures Inc. ("Warner"), Parachute Properties and Parachute Press, Inc., and their respec
   subsidiaries and affiliates, officers, directors, shareholders, employees, agents, attorneys, and other representatives and their imm
   ate families (individually and collectively, "Parachute"), Dualstar Entertainment Group, LLC, and its subsidiaries and affiliates, offi
   directors, shareholders, employees, agents, attorneys, and other representatives and their immediate families (individually and co
   tively, "Dualstar"), and their respective parent companies, affiliates, subsidiaries, advertising, promotion and fulfillment agencies,
   the persons with whom each of the above are domiciled. All applicable federal, state and local laws and regulations apply. Offer
   where prohibited or restricted by law.

4. **Odds of Winning.** Odds of winning depend on the total number of entries received. **Approximately 300,000 sweepsta
   announcements published.** All prizes will be awarded. Winners will be randomly drawn on or about **May 1, 2004,**
   HarperCollins, whose decision is final. Potential winners will be notified by mail and will be required to sign and return an affidav
   eligibility and release of liability within 14 days of notification. Prizes won by minors will be awarded to parent or legal guardian
   must sign and return all required legal documents. By acceptance of their prize, winners consent to the use of their nar
   photographs, likeness, and biographical information by HarperCollins, Parachute, Dualstar, and for publicity purposes without fu
   compensation except where prohibited.

5. **Grand Prize.** 100 Grand Prize Winners each will win one pair of theater passes to see Mary-Kate Olsen and Ashley Olsen's
   feature film *New York Minute* in winner's city. Approximate combined retail value of prizes totals $2000.00.

6. **Prize Limitations.** All prizes will be awarded. Only one prize will be awarded per individual, family, or household. Prizes are
   transferable and cannot be sold or redeemed for cash. No cash substitute is available. Any federal, state, or local taxes are the res
   sibility of the winner. Sponsor may substitute prize of equal or greater value, if necessary, due to availability.

7. **Additional terms:** By participating, entrants agree a) to the official rules and decisions of the judges, which will be final in
   respects; and to waive any claim to ambiguity of the official rules and b) to release, discharge, and hold harmless HarperCol
   Warner, Parachute, Dualstar, and their respective parent companies, affiliates, subsidiaries, employees and representatives and adverti
   promotion and fulfillment agencies from and against any and all liability or damages associated with acceptance, use, or misus
   any prize received or participation in any sweepstakes-related activity or participation in this sweepstakes.

8. **Dispute Resolution.** Any dispute arising from this Sweepstakes will be determined according to the laws of the State of New Y
   without reference to its conflict of law principles, and the entrants consent to the personal jurisdiction of the State and Federal co
   located in New York County and agree that such courts have exclusive jurisdiction over all such disputes.

9. **Winner Information.** To obtain the name of the winners, please send your request and a self-addressed stamped enve
   (residents of Vermont may omit return postage) to New York Minute Free Tickets Winners, c/o HarperEntertainment, 10 East 5
   Street, New York, NY 10022 by **June 1, 2004.**

10. Sweepstakes Sponsor: HarperCollins Publishers, Inc.

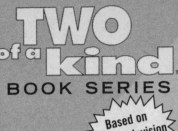

mary-kateandashley™
fragrances

jasmine
spice

juicy
peach
freesia

Real Scents for Real Girls®

www.mary-kateandashley.com

mary-kateandashley
Year of Celebration!
Fashion Dolls

"We're the Class of 2004!
Our senior year is going
to be a blast!"

Graduation Celebration
"From prom to graduation, this will be the best year of our lives!"

Senior year
stylish fashions.

"Look for our
fashion dolls
celebrating our
birthday and join
in the fun!"

Real Dolls for Real Girls®

www.mary-kateandashley.com

DUALSTAR
CONSUMER PRODUCTS

MATTEL

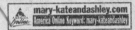

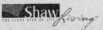

mary-kate olsen
ashley olsen
eugene levy
new york minute
In Theaters May 7th
www.newyorkminutemovie.com
WARNER BROS. PICTURES